THIS BOOK
BELONGS TO

- - - - - - - - - -

To Stella, Marianne and Hannah. I love and appreciate you.
Thanks for thirty years of friendship! – Ems x

For Giacomo, let's go! – GC

Special thanks to Lindsey, Augusta and Paul – LDB

Published by Little Door Books 2019
This edition published 2019

ISBN: 978-1-9999556-1-8

Text copyright © Emily Dodd 2019
Illustrations copyright © Giulia Cregut 2019

A CIP catalogue record for this book is available from the British Library.

mail@littledoorbooks.co.uk
www.littledoorbooks.co.uk
twitter: @littledoorbooks

CRIME SQUIRREL INVESTIGATORS

The naughty nut thief

Emily Dodd   Giulia Cregut

"Slow down!" shouted Charlie.

"You'll never catch me!" said Rosie.

But Charlie wasn't in the mood for catching.
"I'm hungry," he said.

"You're always hungry!" said Rosie.
"Come on!"
Charlie followed her through the forest
until...

...they reached the bottom of a tall pine tree. "Can you keep a secret?" whispered Rosie. "Yes!" said Charlie. He hoped the secret might be something to do with food.

"Oh no!" said Rosie.
She was furious!
"Who's eaten all of my nuts?"

"Don't worry, Rosie. There are still a few left.
I'll help you find some more," said Charlie.

"I don't want more!" said Rosie.
"I want to catch the thief!"

"We're going to be Crime Squirrel Investigators," said Rosie. "Let's look at the evidence. What's our main clue, Charlie?"

"The hazelnut shells?" suggested Charlie.

SUSPECTS

"Exactly!" said Rosie. "The naughty nut thief split them in half. Grab some hazelnuts, Charlie, and let's go."

POLICE LINE DO NOT CROSS

Their first suspect was
    Dora the Dormouse.
Rosie dropped a nut by the door.
She knocked three times and
then they hid.

DORA

Dora was delighted. "BREAKFAST!"
She nibbled the nutshell, turning
it in her paws.
"DELICIOUS!" She popped the
nut into her mouth.

"BEDTIME!"
Dora disappeared indoors,
leaving the evidence behind.

DORA

"Look, Charlie. A smooth round hole,"
said Rosie. "What do we know about the
naughty nut thief?"
"They split the shell in half," said Charlie.
"So Dora's not the nut thief."

"Look! A suspicious green shell…"

I AM NOT A NUT!

"Rosie," said Charlie, "I need to tell you something."

"Not now, Charlie, I can hear tapping," said Rosie.

"Let's go and investigate!"

Tappy the woodpecker was so busy tapping that he didn't hear Rosie sneak up behind him.

She rolled the nut towards him and scampered off.

Tappy stopped tapping. "A HAZELNUT!"
He shoved the nut into a hole.

TAP TAP TAP TAP TAP... BANG!

The hazelnut exploded!
"HAPPY TAPPY!" He flew off
with the nut in his beak.

"Look!" said Rosie. "Tiny pieces of exploded nutshell!
What does that tell us?"
"It tells us that Tappy's not the nut thief," said Charlie.

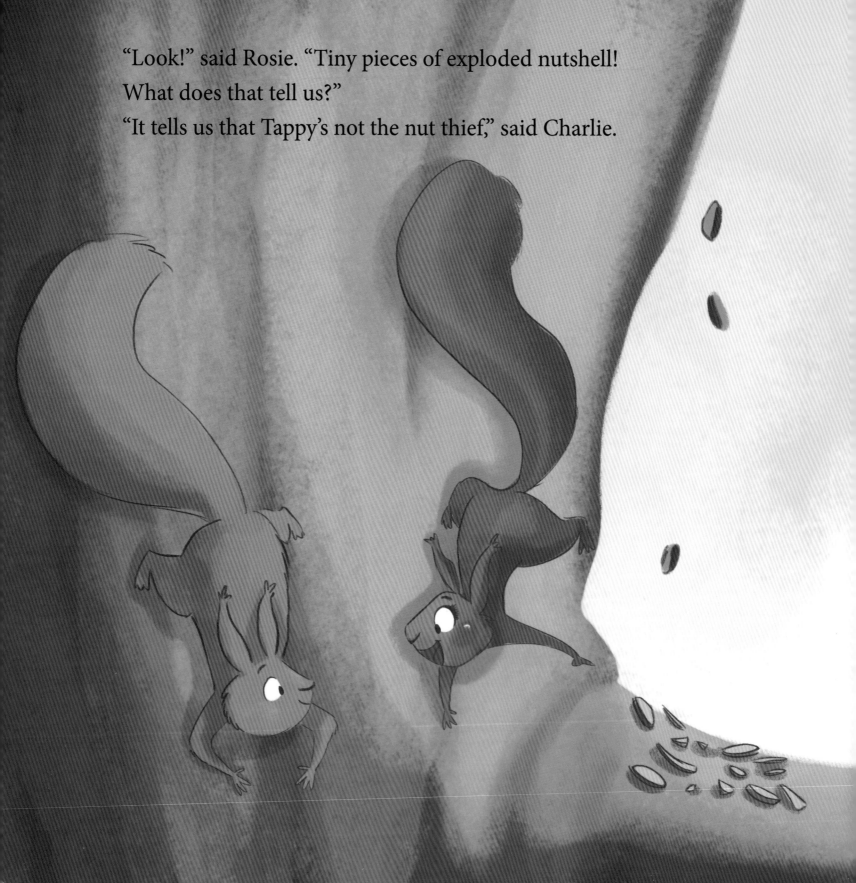

"Look! A suspicious prickly ball," said Rosie.

I AM NOT A BALL, AND I EAT BUGS!

"Rosie," said Charlie, "I really need to tell you something."

"Not now, Charlie," said Rosie. "I can hear squeaking. Let's go!"

"I should have guessed," said Rosie.
"It's Squeaker the wood mouse."
She bounced a nut to Squeaker's door
and then she and Charlie hid.
They didn't have long to wait.

LOVELY NUT!

Squeaker nibbled the nutshell and
threw it out of the window.

"Good catch, Charlie!" said Rosie.

The two investigators examined the evidence.
"Look. It's a little like Dora's shell but Squeaker has left
teeth marks in it," said Rosie.
"So Squeaker's not the nut thief either," said Charlie.

Rosie sighed.

"The investigation is over, Charlie. I'd like you to keep the last hazelnut.
Thank you for being my friend and a brilliant Crime Squirrel Investigator.
You must be hungry."

But Charlie wasn't hungry.

He slowly split the nut shell in half.
Rosie stared.
"I tried to tell you, Rosie, I didn't know
they were your nuts," said Charlie. Rosie was furious!
"You're the nut thief!" she shouted. She turned and ran.

And this time
Charlie didn't follow her.

Charlie felt terrible. He wanted to show Rosie how sorry he was.
So he made a plan, and spent all night working hard.

BEE TREE

BIG LAKE

SECRET NUT STORE

ROSIE HOUSE

N
W E
S

DORA HOUSE

PICNIC PARK

TAPPY HOUSE

SQUEAKER HOUSE

The next morning Rosie woke up surrounded by hazelnuts. She had never seen so many!
Charlie was waiting outside.
He had written her a message.

THE END